READING CORNER

What's in the Barn?

A humorous story
in a familiar setting

First published in 2006 by
Franklin Watts
338 Euston Road
London
NW1 3BH

Franklin Watts Australia
Hachette Children's Books
Level 17/207 Kent Street
Sydney
NSW 2000

A CIP catalogue record for this book is available
from the British Library.

ISBN 0 7496 6564 5 (hbk)
ISBN 0 7496 6565 3 (pbk)

Series Editor: Jackie Hamley
Series Advisors: Dr Barrie Wade, Dr Hilary Minns
Design: Peter Scoulding

Printed in China

What's in the Barn?

Written by
A.H. Benjamin

Illustrated by
O'Kif

W
FRANKLIN WATTS
LONDON•SYDNEY

A.H. Benjamin

"It was fun writing this story. Even I didn't know what was going to happen at the end!"

O'Kif

"From my studio near Buenos Aires in Argentina, I see lots of trees and birds. I can also see my five dogs. The dog in this story looks a lot like my dog 'Brownie'."

All was quiet on the farm.

Suddenly, there was a piercing squawk. Rooster scuttled out of the barn, his feathers flying everywhere.

"It's HORRIBLE!" he wailed,
trembling all over.

Rooster flew to the highest roof
of the farm and would not come
down again.

The other animals were puzzled.
"What's in the barn?" they
wondered. "It must be quite scary!"

"It must be a mouse," said Cat.

"I'll chase it away!"

Cat strolled to the barn.

Her tail twitching, she crept inside.

All was quiet on the farm.

Suddenly, there was a chilling yowl, and Cat shot out of the barn, her fur sticking up like spikes.

"It's SHOCKING!" she gasped, hardly able to get the words out of her mouth. Cat zipped to an empty barrel and dived into it.

"It can't be a mouse," said Dog.

"It must be a fox. I'll deal with it!"

14

Dog padded to the barn.

Baring his teeth, he sneaked inside.

All was quiet on the farm.

Suddenly, there was a piteous yelp, and Dog scampered out of the barn, his tail between his legs.

"It's DREADFUL!" he stammered,
pale as a sheet. Dog sprinted to his
kennel and hid in there.

"It can't be a fox," said Pig.

"It must be a snake. I'll see to it!"

And he trotted to the barn.

Shaking his behind, he barged inside.

All was quiet on the farm.

Suddenly, there was an earsplitting squeal, and Pig bolted out of the barn, his nose quivering with fright.

"It's GHASTLY!" he gibbered, looking scared out of his trotters. He raced to his sty and buried his head in mud.

"It can't be a snake," said Cow.

"It must be a spider. I'll scare it off!"

She waddled to the barn. Horns at
the ready, she charged inside.
All was quiet on the farm.

Suddenly, there was a wild moo,
and Cow clattered out of the barn,
her eyes round with terror.

"It's HIDEOUS!" she spluttered, as if she had seen a ghost. Shaking like a leaf, she hid behind the apple tree.

Just then, the farmer's wife came
out of the house, hands on her hips.

She strode straight towards the
barn and stopped outside the door.
"I know you're in there!" she
shouted. "Come out, now!"

From their hiding places, the animals watched, horrified. All was quiet on the farm. Suddenly, the barn door creaked and groaned as it slowly opened.

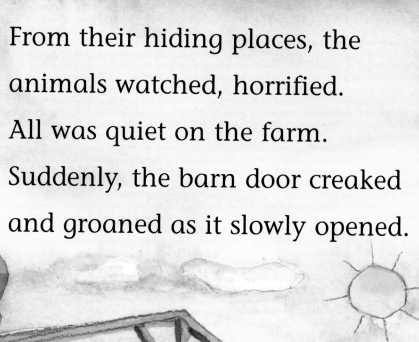

Out came a horrible, shocking,
dreadful, ghastly, hideous ...

... little boy!

"Oh! The state of you!" cried his mother. "Anybody would think you're a monster!"

31

Notes for parents and teachers

READING CORNER has been structured to provide maximum support for new readers. The stories may be used by adults for sharing with young children. Primarily, however, the stories are designed for newly independent readers, whether they are reading these books in bed at night, or in the reading corner at school or in the library.

Starting to read alone can be a daunting prospect. READING CORNER helps by providing visual support and repeating words and phrases, while making reading enjoyable. These books will develop confidence in the new reader, and encourage a love of reading that will last a lifetime!

If you are reading this book with a child, here are a few tips:

1. Make reading fun! Choose a time to read when you and the child are relaxed and have time to share the story.

2. Encourage children to reread the story, and to retell the story in their own words, using the illustrations to remind them what has happened.

3. Give praise! Remember that small mistakes need not always be corrected.

READING CORNER covers three grades of early reading ability, with three levels at each grade. Each level has a certain number of words per story, indicated by the number of bars on the spine of the book, to allow you to choose the right book for a young reader:

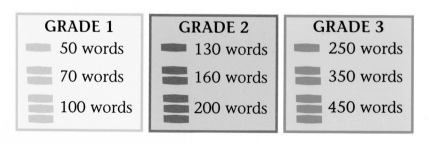

GRADE 1	GRADE 2	GRADE 3
50 words	130 words	250 words
70 words	160 words	350 words
100 words	200 words	450 words